VALENTINE *Princess*

Books about
PRINCESS MIA

The Princess Diaries

THE PRINCESS DIARIES, VOLUME II:
Princess in the Spotlight

THE PRINCESS DIARIES, VOLUME III:
Princess in Love

THE PRINCESS DIARIES, VOLUME IV:
Princess in Waiting

Valentine Princess:
A PRINCESS DIARIES BOOK (VOLUME IV AND A QUARTER)

THE PRINCESS DIARIES, VOLUME IV AND A HALF:
Project Princess

THE PRINCESS DIARIES, VOLUME V:
Princess in Pink

THE PRINCESS DIARIES, VOLUME VI:
Princess in Training

The Princess Present:
A PRINCESS DIARIES BOOK (VOLUME VI AND A HALF)

THE PRINCESS DIARIES, VOLUME VII:
Party Princess

Sweet Sixteen Princess:
A PRINCESS DIARIES BOOK (VOLUME VII AND A HALF)

♡

Illustrated by Chesley McLaren

Princess Lessons:
A PRINCESS DIARIES BOOK

Perfect Princess:
A PRINCESS DIARIES BOOK

Holiday Princess:
A PRINCESS DIARIES BOOK

MEG CABOT

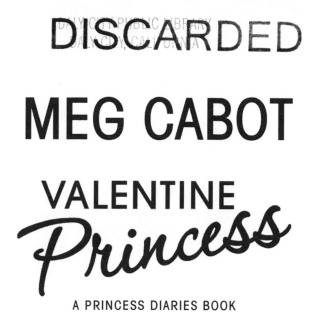

VALENTINE *Princess*

A PRINCESS DIARIES BOOK

HarperCollins*Publishers*

J

Library of Congress Cataloging-in-Publication Data
Cabot, Meg.
  Valentine princess : a princess diaries book / Meg Cabot.— 1st ed.
      p.   cm.
  Summary: Sixteen-year-old Mia finds an old diary and enjoys reading
what she wrote about her first Valentine's Day with Michael.
  ISBN-13: 978-0-06-084718-0 (alk. paper)
  ISBN-10: 0-06-084718-2 (alk. paper)
  [1. Princesses—Fiction. 2. Valentine's Day—Fiction. 3. Diaries—
Fiction. 4. New York (N.Y.)—Fiction. 5. Humorous stories.] I. Title.
PZ7.C11165Val 2006   2006020178
[Fic]—dc22   CIP
                                                               AC

1 2 3 4 5 6 7 8 9 10
❖
First Edition

ACKNOWLEDGMENTS

Many thanks to Beth Ader, Jennifer Brown,
Barbara Cabot, Michele Jaffe, Laura Langlie,
Abigail McAden, and my Valentine,
Benjamin Egnatz.

"You don't know that you are saying these things to a princess, and that if I chose I could wave my hand and order you to execution. I only spare you because I am a princess."

A LITTLE PRINCESS
Frances Hodgson Burnett

ME, A PRINCESS???? YEAH, RIGHT.
A Screenplay by Mia Thermopolis
(first draft)

Scene 44

INT/DAY—The extremely messy bedroom of a teenage
girl, with virtually floor-to-ceiling windows looking out
over a fire escape and inner courtyard. A large yellow
CAT sits on top of the radiator, his tail swishing. A girl
(sixteen-year-old MIA THERMOPOLIS), trembling on
the verge of womanhood, is frantically looking for
something. Her mother (HELEN THERMOPOLIS), a
strikingly attractive woman in her late thirties, appears
in the doorway.

HELEN
Mia! The limo's waiting! Hurry up!

MIA
I can't find my journal! How can I go to

Genovia for the summer if I don't have my
journal?

HELEN leans down and pulls a black-and-white
Mead composition notebook from where it's gotten
wedged between MIA's bed and the wall.

                    HELEN

Isn't this it?

                    MIA

(taking notebook and flipping through it)
No, Mom. This is an old one. This one is from—
Hey! This one is from way back in my
freshman year, a year and a half ago! I've been
looking all over for this! Gosh, I feel like it was
a DECADE ago that the stuff in this journal
went on. I mean, so much has happened since
then. I'll be starting my junior year when I get
back from Genovia at the end of this summer.
God, it's like I'm a totally different person now,
you know? I mean, I'm writing actual PLAYS

now instead of novels. I'm so much older and more sophisticated and—OH MY GOD, THIS IS THE JOURNAL IN WHICH I WROTE ABOUT MY FIRST VALENTINE'S DAY WITH MICHAEL AS A COUPLE!!!!! OH MY GOD, I CAN'T BELIEVE I LOST THIS!!!!! I CAN'T WAIT TO READ IT!!!! EEEEEEEEEEEEE!!!!

Today when I walked into my princess lessons with
Grandmère after school, there was this totally
creepy-looking guy occupying the pink brocade
settee where I normally sit (because it's nearest the
bowl of sugared almonds that I sneak whenever
Grandmère isn't looking, even though they aren't
actually that good, like not candy- or chocolate-
coated or anything, but beggars can't be choosers,
and why do old people always have such sucky candy,
anyway?), and I was all, "Who are you?" because
this dude had on one of those monochromatic tie-
and-shirt thingies, like a TV talk show host or
mafioso might wear, and that is not the kind of
person you'd expect to see sitting in a dowager
princess's living room suite at the Plaza. I mean, not
to be pejorative. But it's true.

Then Grandmère came out in a blue feather-
trimmed wrap, like she was the Queen Mum and not
the princess's grandmum, and was all, "Oh, good,

Amelia, I'm so glad you're here. Meet Dr. Steve," and I was like, "Whaty who?" and she was all, "HOW DARE YOU SPEAK THAT WAY TO MY ASTROLOGIST???"

So yeah. Grandmère has an astrologist.

I will admit, I'm pretty worried because, of course, I thought of Rasputin—you know, that guy who was, like, "spiritual advisor" (aka mystic oracle) to the Russian royal family, before they all ended up getting shot by their angry populace. Not necessarily because of Rasputin, but the czar's subjects did kind of lose respect for him because he and his wife were listening to the advice of a dude who collected hair from virgins as a hobby.

Obviously, this didn't happen with Nancy Reagan, who was getting advice from astrologist Jeane Dixon, but that's just because Jeane Dixon's hobby was playing golf.

Anyway, I guess Dr. Steve isn't like Rasputin. I mean, he doesn't have a beard—in fact, he barely had any hair at all, being mostly bald. And he was wearing a suit, not monk's robes.

Still, I didn't like it much when he pointed at me and went, "Don't tell me! Let me guess! This is Her Royal Highness, Princess Amelia!"

Which made Grandmère clap her hands and do a jig, practically.

"Yes!" she cried. "You're right! He's amazing! Isn't he amazing, Amelia?"

I don't see what's so amazing about it, since he'd heard Grandmère say my name when I walked in.

Plus, it's not like a picture of my face isn't plastered all over the cover of *Teen People* every month. But whatever.

"Tell us what you've learned about Amelia, Doctor," Grandmère said, plopping herself down on one of the matching pink brocade chairs and snapping her fingers at me in her time-honored signal for *Fix me a Sidecar. Now.* "I gave him your birth date and time yesterday, Amelia, and Dr. Steve promised to read the results this afternoon, when you could be here to hear them."

"Um, that's okay," I said, as I headed for the bar. "I'm good. I don't need my fortune told."

Particularly by someone named *Dr. Steve*.

"Dr. Steve doesn't tell *fortunes*, Amelia," Grandmère said, all scornfully. "He examines the positions of celestial bodies in the heavens at the time of someone's birth, and interprets the meaning of that placement to come up with an educated prediction about the future course of events in the subject's life. For instance, Dr. Steve believes I myself am currently in grave danger of incurring grievous bodily harm—"

"Assassination attempt?" I asked hopefully, as I mixed her brandy and Cointreau. Maybe there was more to this Rasputin thing than I thought.

But Grandmère just ignored me. "And will soon be pursued by an ardent suitor. Isn't that correct, Dr. Steve?"

"I definitely see danger for you, Your Highness," Dr. Steve said, looking gravely at my grandmother. "As well as a marriage proposal."

"I'm quite positive it's that odious Lord Crenshaw," Grandmère said, as I handed her her drink. "He's been *quite* persistent in asking to escort me to the charity ball the contessa is hosting for the

American Heart Association on Valentine's Day. Now, Dr. Steve. About Amelia—"

"I don't want to know!" I yelled. Because, seriously, who wants to know their future? Not that I believe in astrology, but, you know, SOME of it is accurate. I mean, like the part about how Capricorns and Tauruses get along so well. Because how else can you explain why Michael Moscovitz, who is the most intelligent and gorgeous senior in the whole school (well, unless you're blind, like everyone who thinks JOSH RICHTER is the most intelligent and gorgeous senior in the whole school), would be going out with a lowly, flat-chested freshman like me? It would be like if Josh Hartnett suddenly started dating Little Debbie, of snack cake fame.

Mmmm, Little Debbies.

But Dr. Steve had already pulled out my chart, and was saying things like, "Her Royal Highness, the princess Mia, is gifted with uncanny insight and takes great pleasure in nature and all living things—"

"Ah!" I cried, trying to get away, only to trip over Rommel, who was cowering in his fur-lined basket by

Grandmère's magazine rack. "No! Don't tell me!"

"She is tremendously persistent, particularly with her affections—"

"Don't say another word!" I was trying to untangle myself from Rommel, but it was hard because he kept darting from one side of his basket to the other. It's a very big basket.

"And that's why her longest-lasting partnership will be with a generous, caring Leo—"

Suddenly, I froze.

"A LEO?" I screamed from the floor. "That's not possible! Michael is a Capricorn!"

"Well, obviously, Amelia," Grandmère said, all primly, taking a sip of her Sidecar, "Michael isn't who you're meant to end up with. What else, Dr. Steve?"

But I stopped listening after that. Because I knew then that Dr. Steve was a charlatan. Oh, he may not dress in monk's robes or have a beard or collect the hair of virgins, but he's no more a mystic oracle than Rasputin ever was.

Because any astrologer who can't interpret from

my star chart that Michael Moscovitz and I are meant to be together forever is a hack.

Or possibly, receiving a kickback from my grandmother, who can't stand Michael because he's not a royal or, even worse, super rich, and so therefore, in her eyes, not a worthy consort for her granddaughter.

I did thank Dr. Steve politely for letting me know I'm destined to do great things when I take over the throne of Genovia, just to be polite. But the truth is, any palm reader off the street could have predicted *that*. I mean, what with my plan to convert the palace into a giant animal shelter, and all.

Jeesh.

I wonder how much money Grandmère has given this fraud. Maybe I should call my dad. I mean, the last thing we need right now is a coup attempt by a populace alienated by Grandmère's profligate spending. Dad's still having a hard enough time calming parliament down about the parking meter controversy I inadvertently started over winter break.

Who knew a bunch of cabinet members could be

so touchy? You'd think they'd be a little more grateful. It's only a matter of time until the constant barrage of tourists from U.S. cruise ships completely destroys Genovia's fragile infrastructure. We've got to start seeking revenue elsewhere, and phase out the cruise ships, or Genovia's going to start sinking, just like Venice.

God, being a princess is *hard*.

Tuesday, February 11, 10 p.m., the loft

Okay, so it was a mistake to IM Tina Hakim Baba and tell her what Dr. Steve said. I mean, I only told her because I thought it was funny, and Tina needs cheering up these days because Valentine's is only three days away and she still doesn't have anyone to exchange cards and Whitman's Samplers with, let alone someone to give her a genuine simulated ruby-encrusted heart pendant from Kay Jewelers (Every Kiss Begins with Kay), since Dave Farouq El-Abar dumped her for a girl named Jasmine, who has turquoise braces (and they didn't even last. Tina said she saw him at Serendipity 3 last weekend sharing a frozen hot chocolate with some girl with no braces and a blow-out).

Anyway, I expected her to be all, "Don't listen to Dr. Steve! He's wrong!" Only that's not how she reacted.

ILUVROMANCE: Seriously, Mia, you have to DO something. Dr. Steve is one of America's premier astrologists! He correctly predicted that 'NSync would break up!

FTLOUIE: Well, if he's that good, I guess there's nothing I can do, is there? Except lie back and accept my fate.

I was totally joking. I forgot that sarcasm is usually totally lost on Tina.

ILUVROMANCE: No!!! That's the WORST thing you could do!!!! What is wrong with you, Mia? You've got to FIGHT!!! FIGHT FOR THE MAN YOU LOVE.

FTLOUIE: Tina, how can I fight for the man I love when I don't even know what I'm fighting against? I mean, not that I believe anything Dr. Steve said has any merit. Don't forget, he says someone's going to propose to Grandmère. Who'd be stupid enough to do THAT?

ILUVROMANCE: Your grandfather, for one. Listen, all this means is that you have to be REALLY careful. Don't give Michael any reason to dump you—the way I did with Dave.

FTLOUIE: Tina! You did not give Dave a reason to dump you! He just dumped you because he's an immature jerk!

ILUVROMANCE: No, Mia. Enough time has passed since our breakup for me to see now where I went wrong. I let Dave slip through my fingers by trying to play it cool, since he was so afraid of commitment. But I see now what I should have done was give him a REASON to WANT TO COMMIT to me.

FTLOUIE: You mean like ... SLEEP WITH HIM???? But, Tina, you promised you and I would be the last virgins at AEHS! I thought we were saving ourselves until the night of our senior prom!!!!

ILUVROMANCE: Of course that's not what I mean,

Mia! There are lots of ways to get a boy to want to commit to you without having to resort to THAT. I mean by showing him that you care in OTHER ways. Like, well, for instance, what are you and Michael doing for Valentine's Day?

FtLouie: Um. I don't know. We haven't talked about it.

Iluvromance: YOU HAVEN'T TALKED ABOUT IT??? THE MOST ROMANTIC HOLIDAY OF THE YEAR???? YOUR FIRST VALENTINE'S DAY EVER WITH AN ACTUAL BOYFRIEND, AND YOU HAVEN'T TALKED ABOUT WHAT YOU'RE GOING TO DO FOR IT?????

FtLouie: No. I guess that's bad, huh? Maybe I should get him a card. . . .

Iluvromance: Not just a card, Mia. Don't you see? This Valentine's Day has special meaning for the both of you, because it's your first as a couple. If you don't plan it exactly right—a romantic dinner, exchange of Valentine's Day gifts, a kiss—Dr. Steve's prediction will come true FOR SURE, and you'll end up with some Leo Boy.

FᴛLᴏᴜɪᴇ: VALENTINE'S GIFT???? I just got done being grounded for stealing those moon rocks for Michael's birthday. What am I going to come up with to give him for VALENTINE'S DAY???? What do girls even GIVE guys for Valentine's Day???? Aren't THEY the ones who are supposed to give US stuff?

Iʟᴜᴠʀᴏᴍᴀɴᴄᴇ: For your first Valentine's Day as a couple, you should give him SOMETHING. Like a book. Or a sweater.

FᴛLᴏᴜɪᴇ: A SWEATER??? DOES IT HAVE TO BE CASHMERE???? Because I'm totally broke. I spent all my allowance on new vegan Doc lookalikes from Pangea.

ILUVROMANCE: I was just using a sweater as an example. What about a CD?

FTLOUIE: Tina, he's a MUSICIAN. When he wants a CD, he goes out and buys it. There's nothing Michael wants that he doesn't have. Except moon rocks. And I already got him those.

ILUVROMANCE: Well, there has to be SOMETHING. Look, I'll think about it and get back to you. But I can't stress enough to you how important this is, Mia. Especially in light of what Dr. Steve said. You have to make this first Valentine's Day with Michael perfect, or you'll end up with Leo Boy. Whoever he is. Or, worse, you'll end up alone. Like me.

FTLOUIE: Tina! Don't worry! Your Valentine is out there somewhere! We just have to find him for you.

ILUVROMANCE: No, Mia, it's all right. All the best guys are taken. I'm all right, really. I'm going to use this Valentine's Day to celebrate my romance with ME. Because you have to learn to love yourself before you can truly love anyone else.

FtLouie: True!

Poor Tina. I HATE that stupid Dave. He better hope he doesn't run into me anytime soon. Lars got a new taser for Christmas, and he's been itching to try it out on someone.

God. Why does everything have to be so COMPLICATED? Just when I thought things were starting to go fine for a change, some stupid psychic has to come around and ruin it.

That is just so my luck.

And as usual, it's all Grandmère's fault. Why'd she have to go and hire a stupid astrologist anyway? Why can't she hire a chiropractor, like a normal grandma?

Wednesday, February 12, Algebra

So I tried to be all subtle in the car on the way to school. You know, about the whole Valentine's Day thing? After Michael and Lilly got into the limo—and I got over how cute Michael looked with his neck all newly shaved and pink and gorgeous . . . God, it is totally UNFAIR that anyone should look that good in the morning—I was all, "So, Lilly. What are you and Boris doing for Valentine's Day?" You know, super casually, and everything.

And Lilly was like, "Valentine's Day? Are you on crack?"

"Um." I wish Lilly wouldn't ask me if I'm on crack in front of her brother. I mean, I know Michael knows I don't use drugs. But it's, like, totally rude. "No. It's coming up, you know. Friday."

I thought this was kind of sly, how I threw in that Valentine's Day was on Friday, to kind of remind Michael? Only I didn't say it TO Michael. I said it to Lilly. So that was cool.

"I know when the fourteenth day of February falls, Mia," Lilly said, all sarcastically. "What I meant was, since when do you celebrate a holiday that is essentially an invention of the greeting card and floral industries, who got together one day and decided to devise yet another holiday to make the loveless feel bad?"

"Um," I said again. "Actually, Saint Valentine was a real priest who kept marrying soldiers even after the Roman emperor instructed him not to, because the emperor felt single men made better fighters. So the emperor had Valentine thrown in jail, where he fell in love with the prison keeper's daughter, and wrote her love notes signed 'Your Valentine,' which is why today we send Valentines to our loved ones."

"Um," Lilly said, imitating me—and not in a very nice way—"actually, Valentine was just a man who helped hide Christians from the Romans, a crime for which he was discovered and then clubbed to death on February fourteenth."

"Actually, you're both wrong," Michael said,

looking amused. "Ancient Romans celebrated the goddess Juno on February fourteenth, and Lupercalia—a popular feast starting in the third century that honored the god Lupercus, protector of sheep from wolves—the next day. On the eve of the fifteenth, the names of boys and girls would be drawn, and they were supposed to be linked for the year."

My boyfriend is so smart!!!!!!!!!!! Also, his neck smells good. Not that I got to smell it until later, when we got out of the car. But when I did, it smelled good. REALLY good. I realize it's just the pheromones Michael gives off that elevate the serotonin levels in my brain, thus making me feel all nice and relaxed when he's around, like we learned in Bio.

But I really, really like Michael's pheromones. They are WAY better than some Leo Boy's pheromones. I'm sure of it.

"Later," Michael went on, "Christian priests, in an attempt to rid the land of heathen practices, changed the name of the feast from Lupercalia to Valentine's Day, and matched children's names to saints, so they could try to emulate the life of the saint whose name they were paired with. But being paired up with a member of the opposite sex proved more popular."

"God," Lilly said. "I guess so. Would you want to have to go around emulating some guy who got clubbed and beheaded?"

"WHATEVER." I couldn't believe how the conversation had gotten sidetracked. *"What are you and Boris doing to celebrate Valentine's Day, Lilly?"*

"I already told you," Lilly said. "NOTHING. I don't take part in barbaric pagan rituals. I've never celebrated Valentine's Day. You *know* that, Mia. I mean, have I ever given you a Valentine? Except when some dumb teacher MADE us sit there and make Valentines, because it meant she could sneak off for half an hour to smoke while we were doing busywork, another example of how inferior our educational system is to the rest of the world's?"

"Well." I was genuinely shocked to hear all this. "No. But I mean, this is your first Valentine's Day with an actual boyfriend. Aren't you even going to get Boris a card?"

"And contribute some of my hard-earned income to the already burgeoning coffers of Hallmark, who by the way barely pay a living wage to the artists who work for them? Not likely."

Which is when the limo pulled up, and we had to get out of the car.

But I wouldn't let that daunt me. Because as we went into school, I said to Michael, "But *you* don't feel that way about Valentine's Day, do you, Michael? That it's a barbaric pagan ritual?"

"What?" Michael looked amused. "No. But I agree that it's become a gross commercial by-product of the card manufacturing, floral, and candy industries, and that the best way to protest that kind of materialism is to refuse to take part in it. Have fun in Algebra."

Then he kissed me—causing my oxytocin levels to rise—and ran off to his own class.

I'm pretty sure when Tina hears about this, she isn't going to take it as a good sign.

I mean about the Valentine's thing. Not about my oxytocin levels.

Wednesday, February 12,
Gifted and Talented

I was right! Today at lunch—which was the first time I got to talk to Tina all day—when I told her what Lilly and Michael said, she was like, "That's bad, Mia."

We were standing in the jet line to get Nutty Royales for dessert, while Lilly and everyone else were back at the lunch table. So it wasn't like we had to worry about anyone overhearing us. Well, except other people in the lunch line. But there was no one behind us and the only person in front of us was the Guy Who Hates It When They Put Corn in the Chili, so that didn't matter.

"I know," I said. "But what am I supposed to do? Michael's a Valentine Hater."

"You've got to cure him," Tina said. "He may hate Valentine's Day only because he's never actually experienced a good one."

"Neither have I," I pointed out.

"That's all the more reason why you have to work

to make this, your first Valentine's Day together, the most special one ever."

"But I told you, Tina," I said, "I don't have any money."

"You don't need to spend money to make a gift special," Tina said. "That's the part Lilly and Michael are right about. Don't let the greeting card and candy companies—and jewelers and florists—make you think that unless you purchase something spectacular for your loved one, you obviously don't love them very much. Homemade gifts are more meaningful, because they truly come from the heart. Why don't you *make* Michael a Valentine?"

"Oh, right," I said. "You mean because I'm so crafty? Remember when I got that second-degree burn putting my tile in the oven at Our Name Is Mud? Besides, it's going to be lame if I give him something and he doesn't give me anything. It's just going to make him think his girlfriend is so weak, she's succumbed to the pressure of a commercial holiday."

"No, it won't," Tina said, looking shocked.

"He'll think it's sweet."

It was right then that Lana Weinberger came up behind us in line, talking really loudly into her cell phone (even though we aren't supposed to use them in school), going, "That's right, Trish, it turns out I can't make the concert Friday after all. Josh finally got his act together and asked me to go with him to One if by Land, Two if by Sea, you know, that former carriage house that's been renovated into one of the most romantic restaurants in New York City? Yeah, he reserved the table by the fireplace so the two of us can snuggle. And his dad is making sure we get a bottle of Cristal. It's going to be the most romantic Valentine's Day *ever.*"

It was really hard not to throw up, but somehow Tina and I managed. At least until the Guy Who Hates It When They Put Corn in the Chili was like, "Is there corn in this?" to the lady behind the hot food counter, and she was like, "Yes," and the Guy Who Hates It When They Put Corn in the Chili was like, "Do you have any without corn in it?" and the lady behind the counter was like, "No," and Lana, behind us, lowered her phone and was all, "OH MY GOD, COULD THIS LINE BE GOING ANY SLOWER?"

"God, Lana, relax," I said. Because I really did feel badly for the the Guy Who Hates It When They Put Corn in the Chili, since he'd just been asking a question. "It's not like your Zone bar is going to go bad while you wait," since that was all she was buying.

To which Lana didn't even bother replying, she just got back on her phone and was like, "God, I can't WAIT until I've graduated and don't have to spend all my time with so many CHILDREN," which, good luck to her, isn't going to be for another three and a half years.

But that's not even the worst part. The worst part is when I got to G and T, Boris was all, "Mia, come here," when Lilly was busy showing Mrs. Hill the tiny prosthetic foot she made out of challah for a scene she's shooting for this week's episode of *Lilly Tells It Like It Is* (an exploration of self-mutilation in the pursuit of beauty in cultures throughout history, starting with foot binding in the T'ang Dynasty and leading up to breast augmentation in the modern U.S. adult entertainment field).

So I followed Boris into the supply closet, which is where we force him to practice because otherwise we all get headaches. I had actually never been in there before. But really, I don't see what he's complaining about all the time; it's quite pleasant, except for the lack of natural light. And I happen to enjoy the smell of Pine-Sol.

"So I got this for Lilly for Valentine's Day," Boris said, digging something out of his violin case. "Do you think she'll like it?"

And there, in his hand, was a small velvet box containing—

A genuine simulated ruby-encrusted heart pendant from Kay Jewelers, just like the one Tina had always wanted!

I have to say, the way it sparkled, as it caught the light from the single naked bulb hanging overhead, took my breath away.

"Boris," I said, my heart weeping for him.

Because, of course, I fully know what Lilly is getting him for Valentine's Day: nothing. "It's the most gorgeous necklace ever. She'll LOVE it."

"I hope so," Boris said, looking embarrassed. "I mean, I know she doesn't usually wear things like that. But I thought maybe that's because no one has ever given her anything like this."

I swear, this almost made me burst out crying.

WHO KNEW BORIS PELKOWSKI WAS SUCH A ROMANTIC?????

Wednesday, February 12, 4 p.m., limo on the way home from the Plaza

Today when I got to the Plaza, Grandmère was getting ready to go out, and when she saw me, she was like, "Oh, Amelia! I don't have time today. Go home."

Seriously. Nice way to be greeted by your grandmother, right?

"But what about princess lessons?" I wanted to know. I mean, we're right in the middle of learning how to put on a sari, in the event I am ever gifted with one and have to wear it to a state dinner.

"No time," Grandmère said, as she was drawing on her eyebrows. "Dr. Steve's going to be on *Larry King* tonight, and I promised I'd go to the studio with him for moral support. He's nervous, poor dear."

"You're going WITH him?" I demanded.

"Well, yes, of course," Grandmère said. "Not everyone is used to having cameras and bright lights on them and giving interviews to journalists at the drop of a hat like we are, Amelia."

I liked how she said *we*—because I will NEVER get used to having cameras and bright lights on me, and I hate giving interviews. But still.

"Grandmère," I said. I knew this was going to be touchy. Still, I felt a moral obligation to ask. "Aren't you taking things with this Steve guy—"

"DR. Steve."

"With this DR. Steve guy a little fast? I mean, you only just met him." VIRGIN HAIR. That's all I could think about. In 1977, when they finally knocked down Rasputin's house, they found box after box of HAIR he'd hidden in the walls.

"Amelia." Grandmère stopped rushing around for a minute to glare at me. "Dr. Steve is a genius. When a genius asks you for your help, of course you oblige him. As I've often told you, by spending time in the company of truly gifted people, you yourself will only grow and improve as a person, merely from the acquaintance."

Well, this totally explains why I hang out with Michael so much (I mean, besides the pheromones).

But Dr. Steve, a genius? I don't know. I'm starting to get worried. What if this guy really IS a Rasputin-type character? I wish my dad were in town so I could ask him what he thinks about all this. Because what if Dr. Steve is some type of svengali—you know, one of those charismatic schemers who hypnotizes women into doing his bidding with his charm alone, like that David Koresh dude from that cult in Waco, or all those fundamentalist Mormon guys who get their thirteen-year-old stepdaughters to marry them?

And what if Grandmère becomes some sort of slave to Dr. Steve, and decides to follow him around the globe, like he's her guru?

Whoa. I might never have princess lessons again.

YIPPEE!!!!

No, wait, that's no good. I mean, not about the princess lessons, but about my grandma being bamboozled by some flimflam astrologist. Should I call Dad?

Yeah, I guess I should.

Well, maybe next week. It'll be nice to have the

next few days off from princess lessons so I can concentrate on what I'm going to do about Michael and Valentine's Day.

God. And I thought, once I finally got Michael to fall in love with me, all my problems would be solved. HA!

Wednesday, February 12, 10 p.m., the loft

I just asked Mom what she and Mr. Gianini were doing for Valentine's Day, and she just laughed in an evil way and went, "Nothing."

Mr. Gianini was in the room at the time, sorting laundry, and he looked all hurt and said, "What do you mean, nothing? I'm taking you out!"

Which just caused Mom to raise her feet from where she was resting them on, like, twenty pillows and go, "Not with these swollen ankles, bub."

"Fine, then," Mr. Gianini said. "We'll order in. But we're doing *something* for Valentine's Day, Helen."

And then my mom forgot her pregnancy hormone rage and looked at him all dewy-eyed and went, "Oh, honey," and Mr. G looked all lovey-dovey back at her.

And I had to leave the room really quick before I gagged.

It's so not fair. Even my MOM has a Valentine. And Mr. G, while he may not be a genius, is a really smart guy. How come HE believes in Valentine's Day, and Michael doesn't? WHAT IS WRONG WITH MICHAEL??? Did he have some horrible Valentine's Day experience that scarred him for life? Did he once sustain some hideous paper cut opening a Valentine? That wouldn't stop bleeding? And he ended up in the hospital? And had to get stitches? WHAT IS IT ABOUT VALENTINE'S DAY THAT HE HATES SO MUCH?

Oh, great, his sister is IMing me. Maybe she can help clear this up.

WOMYNRULE: Hey. I need help constructing my diorama depicting the hijra. Can I borrow your old Ken dolls?

FTLOUIE: Is this for your self-mutilation thing?

WOMYNRULE: Yeah. . . .

FTLOUIE: No, you can't borrow my Ken dolls! You're just going to cut pieces off them!

WOMYN RULE: No, I'm not. See, the hijra are eunuchs in India, who've had both their testes and penis removed. They go around blessing brides and grooms at weddings. And you know Ken is totally smooth down there. So he'll be perfect.

FT LOUIE: Oh. Also, gross. Well, I guess in that case, you can borrow them. Can I ask you something, though? Something about Michael?

WOMYN RULE: Can I stop you, much as I might like to?

FT LOUIE: Why does Michael hate Valentine's Day so much?

WOMYN RULE: Oh, God. Not this again.

FT LOUIE: Come on, Lilly, it's our first Valentine's Day together as a couple! MY first Valentine's Day when I actually have a Valentine. And Michael doesn't want any part of it. WHY?????

WomynRule: He told you WHY. He thinks it's a stupid holiday invented by the greeting card companies to take advantage of simple-minded schmos like you.

FtLouie: Mr. G and my mom are doing something for Valentine's Day, and they are not simple-minded schmos.

WomynRule: I meant simple-minded schmo figuratively. Look, Mia, I know how much you want one of those genuine simulated ruby heart pendants from Kay Jewelers (snerk), but Michael isn't the simulated-ruby-heart-pendant type.

I can't believe she mentioned the simulated ruby heart pendant! The one Boris got her! Does she know about it, somehow? Or was she just being sarcastic? Why did she write *snerk* after it? Does she really think they're dorky? What's she going to do when Boris gives her the one he got her? Is she going to *say* snerk out loud? That will break Boris's heart!

FtLouie: I don't see what's wrong with those ruby heart pendants. I think they're pretty!!!! I'd be totally touched if a boy gave me one.

WomynRule: You would. But don't expect one from Michael. He's not the simulated-ruby type. In fact, he's not the Valentine's-Day type. I can't believe you haven't realized that by now.

Not the Valentine's-Day type? What does that even mean? How can someone not be the Valentine's-Day type? Valentine's Day is all about flowers and chocolate and funny cards. Who doesn't like those kinds of things? WHO????

God, what if Dr. Steve's prediction about my ending up with a Leo is right? Because I really don't see how two people with such very different opinions about a holiday could ever end up working it out and staying together. I mean, if I give Michael a Valentine, he'll think I'm a simple-minded schmo. And if he doesn't give me one, I'm going to feel like he's an uncaring jerk (well, I will).

And then some LEO is going to move in and sweep me off my feet!

Why can't Michael see that by refusing to participate in Valentine's Day, he could be threatening our future happiness??????

Thursday, February 13, Algebra

Today, before class, I went up to Mr. G and was like, "Can I talk to you?" and he went, "Mia, if you're about to tell me you didn't finish all the problems at the end of the chapter, when I happen to know you were up until eleven o'clock IMing with Lilly—"

"No, I finished them," I explained hastily. God, it sucks to have to live with your Algebra teacher. "What I wanted to know was, um, have you always believed in Valentine's Day? Or just since you started seeing my mom?"

Mr. G looked at me kind of funny, but he seemed to give the matter some thought. "Well, no, I can't say I have always been a proponent of Valentine's Day. But now that I'm with your mother, I think it's a nice way to acknowledge her and what she means to me."

"See!" I said. "That's how I feel! But Michael is, like, totally anti–Valentine's Day! How can I get him to realize it's a perfectly legitimate holiday?"

"Well," Mr. G said, kind of dryly. "I wouldn't go

so far as to say that Valentine's Day is a perfectly legitimate holiday. But you know, Mia, whether or not you believe in Valentine's Day doesn't really matter. What matters is whether or not you're a good friend to the people you care about, and who care about you."

And I know Mr. G is right. It doesn't matter whether or not Michael believes in Valentine's Day. All that matters is that we care about each other.

But still. WHAT ABOUT LEO BOY????

Thursday, February 13, G&T

Even though it was Thursday, Michael sat with us at lunch today because the Computer Club's meeting was canceled due to three of the members being out with the flu. I think he sort of regretted it though because Lilly was telling us all about how rib removal, with abdominoplasty, is the new up-and-coming thing in the plastic surgery field, and that women seeking an hourglass figure are lining up to have it done, in the false belief that there's a historic precedent for this kind of surgery, because Victorian women used to have it done to achieve their own wasp waists.

Except that this is a lie because surgery in Victorian times was almost always fatal, and if women really HAD had their eleventh and twelfth ribs removed in pursuit of an eighteen-inch waist, they'd have died on the operating table.

I'll admit, it WAS kind of hard to eat my veggie burger after that. I can't wait until her self-mutilation episode is done.

But she still has the Michael Jackson segment to finish.

Anyway, while we were sitting there, who should come up but Judith Gershner, the girl I used to think Michael was in love with. Even though now I know they were just friends, I still feel twinges of jealousy about ol' Judith. I mean, she *is* super smart.

And her boobs are HUGE.

"Michael, you know science fair apps are due today, right?" Judith asked him.

And Michael practically choked on his spaghetti and meatballs and was all, "I forgot!" and Judith was like, "Well, you'd better get your application in by the end of fifth period, or you won't qualify for regionals, and then I won't be able to kick your butt in them," and Michael was all, "I'm on it," and grabbed his backpack.

"Gotta go," he said to me. "You can have my Yodels if you want."

Which was particularly nice of him because he really could have taken the Yodels with him. But he knows how much I love them.

And okay, it isn't a Valentine, but it's pretty darn close.

"He'd lose his head if it wasn't attached to his body," Judith said with a sigh, reaching for Michael's abandoned garlic bread. Which I thought was kind of rude. Not that she was eating his garlic bread, but her implication that Michael isn't very organized. Because he totally is. Well, more than me, anyway.

"Of course the whole thing was started by Hippocrates," we both overheard Lilly saying, "who maintained that the body's humors could be rebalanced by bloodletting, blistering, or purging by vomiting or anal purgatives."

"Ewwww," said Tina and Boris, at the same time.

"Wow," Judith said, impressed. "I should eat lunch with you guys more often."

"It's for her TV show," I explained.

"Oh," Judith said, chewing. "Groovalicious."

It kind of surprised me that she would just sit down and start eating Michael's lunch like that. I mean, hello, he had BITTEN that piece of garlic bread. I don't mind Michael's germs, but it surprised me that Judith, who isn't even his girlfriend, wouldn't mind them, either.

And then I started wondering if there was a REASON she didn't mind them. Like, that maybe she had a crush on Michael or something. Even though supposedly she's seeing some guy from Trinity.

But then, you think a lot of crazy things when you're watching some other girl eat your boyfriend's garlic bread.

So I was like, all conversationally, "So what are you doing for Valentine's Day, Judith?"

And she was all, "Valentine's Day? Are you kidding me? Do people even celebrate that anymore?"

And I looked pointedly around the cafeteria, the walls of which were completely plastered with pink and red hearts and doilies, courtesy of the Pep Club.

"Oh," Judith said, following the direction of my gaze. "Right. Well, I don't know. I guess my boyfriend and I will grab something to eat somewhere. I don't know."

"Is apathy toward Valentine's Day inherent in the senior class, or something?" I asked. "Because Michael has sort of the same attitude about it."

"Well," Judith said. "I mean, it *is* kind of lame. It's like a holiday designed to make you feel bad about yourself. If you do have someone, and they don't get you a Valentine, you feel like crap. And then if you don't have anybody, it's like you're an even bigger loser. So basically, you have to get a card for everyone you know, but then it basically has no meaning, and the people who benefit most are the ones at Hallmark. Personally, I think everybody should just opt out."

Opt out? Opt out of Cupids holding *Be Mine* banners and *I Choo-choo-choose You* train engine Valentines and heart-shaped boxes of chocolate with gooey unidentifiable things in the middle and little candy hearts that taste like chalk but say stuff like *U R Hot* on them?

Is she insane???? Is EVERYONE insane?

Thursday, February 13, French

Mia—Have you talked to Michael about Valentine's Day yet???—Tina

No. I mean, what's the point? He really doesn't believe in it. And Lilly says he thinks people who do are simple-minded schmos.

That's probably just because he's never had a happy one! It's up to you to show him that Valentine's Day can be a wonderful time, full of fun and romance!

Yeah, I'm not so sure about that, Tina. I think I may just kind of forget the whole thing this year.

Aw! Well, if you want to come over to watch a Valentine movie marathon all night with me and Lilly and Ling Su, you're totally welcome to. I'm trying to get Shameeka to come, but, you know. She's got a Valentine's Day date.

What movies are you guys watching?

The best Valentine movies ever!

TINA HAKIM BABA'S TOP FIVE VALENTINE'S DAY MOVIES
(Guaranteed to cheer you up whether you have a Valentine to snuggle up with or not)

Breakfast at Tiffany's—Glamorpuss Holly Golightly is a beautiful party girl who doesn't believe people—or cats—should belong to anyone. Can the cute boy in the apartment next door change all that? Favorite scene: when Audrey Hepburn and George Peppard go looking for Cat in the pouring rain.

Funny Face—Frumpy and bookish, Jo Stockton is hardly supermodel material . . . but photographer Fred Astaire sees the swan beneath the ugly duckling, and soon Jo is in Paris on a whirlwind fashion shoot in which she ends up losing her heart.

Favorite scene: when Audrey Hepburn gets all the new clothes!

Sabrina—Tomboyish Sabrina fears she'll always be just the chauffeur's daughter to rich employer David Larrabee . . . until a makeover transforms her into a chic fashion plate. Favorite scene: when Audrey Hepburn tells William Holden she's named her poodle David!

Charade—Pretty new widow Reggie discovers that her husband has stolen a fortune, and every cad in town—including Cary Grant—thinks she knows where he's hidden it. Favorite scene: when Audrey Hepburn points at the cleft in Cary Grant's chin and wonders aloud, "How do you shave in there?"

My Fair Lady—Pretty flower seller Eliza Doolittle finds herself at the center of a love triangle between the professor who's taught her how to act like a lady and the young gentleman who's fallen

in love with her. Favorite scene: when Audrey
Hepburn goes to the ball.

Um, wow, Tina. That sounds like a pretty good
marathon. But you do realize, don't you, that all
of those movies star Audrey Hepburn?

**Of course! Why shouldn't they? She's the
greatest star who ever lived!**

Well! Good to know! And save some popcorn for
me. I may just join you.

**YAY!!!! I mean, it's not that I WANT you and
Michael to break up—I don't want you to start
going out with some Leo Boy we don't even know.
You and Michael were so meant for each other—
just like Justin and Britney!!!! But it will be more
fun if you can come.**

Thanks, Tina. I know what you mean. Aren't
Britney and Justin just the cutest? They really are

so destined for each other. Sigh.

ODE TO MICHAEL

Oh, Michael, can't you see
You and me were meant to be?
Just like Britney's got her Justin
For you I will always be lustin'.
You're the best I ever had—
I'm your Jennifer, you're my Brad.

Thursday, February 13,
limo on the way home from the Plaza

GRANDMÈRE IS MISSING!!!!

Princess lessons were canceled for the day because NO ONE CAN FIND MY GRANDMOTHER!

SHE'S BEEN DOWAGER-PRINCESS-NAPPED!

Well, okay, not really. I mean, I don't think anyone is holding her for ransom. Because if they were, we'd probably have heard from them already, begging us to please take her off their hands. I truly pity anyone who would try to kidnap Grandmère. First of all, they would probably choke to death from all the secondhand smoke. And if that didn't finish them off, all the criticizing of their kidnapping technique would make them WISH they were dead.

"I have never seen such slipshod handling of an automatic weapon! What's wrong with you? Do you take no pride in your work? A monkey would make a better kidnapper than you!"

Except that I'm pretty sure she hasn't been kidnapped. According to her maid, Dr. Steve came to fetch her after breakfast this morning, and the two of them have been gone all day.

But there've been periodic spottings: They were seen on the *Today Show*, being interviewed by Katie Couric about Dr. Steve's prediction that Prince Charles will give up the throne in order to be allowed to marry Camilla Parker Bowles. And then later they showed up on *Maury*, where Dr. Steve correctly guessed that the real father of a girl named Tiffany's baby was not her husband, Roy, but her husband's son from a previous marriage, Jimmy. Dr. Steve then correctly guessed that Roy would punch Jimmy, which he promptly did.

I wonder if I should call my dad. I mean, this is just not normal. Not the incestuous nature of Tiffany's love life, but the whole Grandmère thing. Grandmère NEVER misses a princess lesson, if she can help it. What other joys does she have in life, besides torturing me for two or three hours? Except for smoking and swilling Sidecars, of course? Oh, and shopping?

On the other hand, if I call Dad, he'll just find

some way to pry Grandmère away from Dr. Steve, and I'll have princess lessons again. What am I, crazy? I don't want to spend any more afternoons learning diplomatic protocol than I have to.

But I kind of don't want to just sit back and let Grandmère make a giant fool of herself over a guy. Especially a guy who might turn out to be a Svengali-David Koresh-Fundamentalist-Mormon-Rasputin type. Remember what happened to the Romanov girls! And Grandmère doesn't wear diamonds on her corsets like they did, so the bullets won't exactly bounce off and ricochet around the room before finally nailing her in the forehead, like they did Anastasia.

Wow, this is, like, a real problem. I really have to think about it. Am I going to be unselfish and rat Grandmère out for her own good? Or selfish and just let her crash and burn?

Hmmmmm . . .

Thursday, February 13, the loft

So I just asked Mom what she would do if a "friend" was making a really bad mistake—would she mind her own business, or tell her what she thought?

And Mom was like, "Mia, is Lilly doing drugs? What kind of drugs? Tell me now. You know, two girls down at NYU died last weekend from doing ecstasy—"

"Whoa. Mom. No. It's not drugs."

"Oh," Mom says, blinking. "Well, then what kind of mistake do you mean?"

But by then I was so freaked I didn't want to talk about it anymore. So I just told her Lilly was thinking about getting her nose pierced, and Mom was like, "Oh my God, that is so 1998," and said she was surprised Lilly would do something so mainstream, but then observed that Lilly might actually look good with a little diamond in her nostril.

Parents. Seriously.

But then before I could escape to my room Mom was like, "What are you and Michael planning on doing tomorrow night for Valentine's Day, honey?"

And I practically burst into tears.

I don't know what came over me. You'd have thought *I* was the pregnant one.

Anyway, I guess she heard my voice break when I said, "Nothing. Michael doesn't believe in Valentine's Day," since she said, all sympathetically, "Well, just because he doesn't believe in Valentine's Day doesn't mean you have to stop believing in it, too."

And I was like, "Yeah, but if I give him a Valentine, he's going to think I'm a giant dork."

And Mom was all, "Oh, honey, Michael would never think anything you did was dorky. He adores you."

"Yeah, but how lame is it to give a Valentine to someone you KNOW isn't going to give you one back?"

"I don't think it's lame at all," Mom said. "In fact, I think that's what Valentine's Day is all about—giving without expecting anything in return. That's true love, if you ask me."

!!!!!!!!!

You know what? For once, I think my mom is right. I don't care what Michael thinks—I'm giving him a Valentine. And if he laughs at me, he laughs at me.

But at least I'll be doing what *I* want for a change, instead of what everyone EXPECTS from me.

Friday, February 14, Algebra

I haven't given it to him yet. I wanted to give it to him first thing this morning, in the limo. But stupid Lilly wouldn't stop talking about how ninety percent of breast implants rupture over time, and how if you're going to get breast implants you need to be prepared to periodically have them replaced or removed, like Pam Anderson.

Which isn't exactly the kind of romantic setting you want when you are about to give someone a Valentine you were up half the night making.

Still, I've already gotten one Valentine—my mom got up early and made me heart-shaped pancakes! I couldn't believe it.

And okay, maybe it is kind of pathetic that my only Valentine so far is from my mom.

But at least I've gotten one!

And I've given one, too . . . to Lars. It's a card I bought at Ho's Deli when he wasn't looking. I couldn't resist, because it has a picture of a heart holding an automatic rifle on the front, and then when you open it, it says, *Valentine . . . I'm gunning for you!* inside.

I don't think I'm exaggerating when I say that Lars got a little teary-eyed over it. He may be six and a half feet of unadulterated, Israeli Army–trained muscle. But inside that size forty-four chest, my bodyguard is just a big softy.

I don't know when I'm going to give Michael his Valentine. He has a make-up Computer Club meeting today at lunch, and then I won't see him again, unless I go over to his place after school—providing princess lessons are canceled again (I'm calling ahead this time).

Please, please let Grandmère's midlife crisis, or whatever this is, be continuing! (As long as she doesn't get hurt, of course. Figuratively or literally.)

Friday, February 14, Health and Safety

OH MY GOD. What did he give you?

SHUT UP.

Seriously. Just show me.

SHUT UP!!!!!

Come on. What is it? I want to see!!!!!

Lilly. No. Pay attention. We are learning a very important lesson today about genital warts. I would think you, in particular, would be fascinated by this subject.

JUST SHOW ME.

Here. Satisfied????

A WHITMAN'S SAMPLER???? KENNY

*SHOWALTER STOPPED BY YOUR LOCKER
TO GIVE YOU A WHITMAN'S SAMPLER
FOR VALENTINE'S DAY?????? MWA HA HA
HA!!!!*

It isn't funny!!!! He did it right in front of
Michael!!!!

*Well, good. There's nothing wrong with letting my
brother know he has a little competition.*

Michael doesn't have any competition for my
affections! He knows I only like Kenny as a
friend.

Yeah, but does KENNY know that?

I've only told him, like, 900,000,000 times. Oh,
God, why did he DO that????

Because he looooooves you. What did the card say?

Bee my Valentine. And there's a picture of a bee.

MWA HA HA HA! Give me one.

No! They're mine!

Oh, COME ON. You don't even like cream-filled chocolate.

I do, too!

You do not. You only like the crunchy toffee ones. Come on, fork one over.

Go get your own stalker to give you candy. Kenny's mine.

Selfish.

Ha! You're one to talk.

What do you mean by that?

Nothing.

No, seriously. Why am I selfish?

What are you going to do if Boris gives you a
Valentine's Day gift? A really nice one?

*He wouldn't dare. We already talked about it. And I
told him I'm opposed to Valentine's Day on ethical
grounds.*

Yeah, well, you Moscovitzes might think you can
tell people what to do. But some of us have minds
of our own.

What is THAT supposed to mean?

Nothing.

*You're psycho. Almost as psycho as your grandmother.
Who I saw on* David Letterman *last night with some
creepy astrologist who was going on about how Tom*

Cruise and Katie Holmes are going to get together.
Like THAT's ever going to happen. I mean, Tom's
WAY too old for Joey!!!!

Okay. I seriously have to do something about
Grandmère. This is getting out of control.

Well, maybe just one more day . . .

Friday, February 14, Lunch

Tina just reminded me of something I forgot: KENNY SHOWALTER IS A LEO!!!!

AAAAAAAAAAHHHHHHHHHHHHHH-HHHHHHHHHH!!!!!!!!!!!!!!!!!!!!!!

Lunch was totally magical today!!!!

Okay, first of all, Tina and I were in front of Lana in the lunch line again, and while we were standing there, Lana's cell phone rang, and she answered it, and was all, "Oh, hi, Josh," in this gross syrupy voice.

And so I looked at Tina and pretended to stick my finger down my throat, you know, like I was barfing. Which cracked Tina up.

But then Lana's voice got all high-pitched and wobbly, and she was like, "What do you mean, you pulled a groin muscle?" and it turned out Josh was calling her from the Cabrini emergency room, which is where he was taken after third period when he could no longer take the excruciating pain in his upper thigh a second longer. Apparently, he'd pulled something at basketball practice the night before, but the throbbing didn't get really bad until Trig class the next day.

Which just goes to show that nothing good ever comes from canceling plans with a girlfriend because suddenly you got a date, the way Lana did to Trish when Josh asked her out. Karma really *is* a bitch.

"Why didn't you apply heat to it immediately?" Lana demanded.

But we never got to hear the answer to that, because I guess that's when Josh broke the news that he had to stay home and ice his groin and wouldn't be able to take Lana to One if by Land, Two if by Sea for their romantic fireside Valentine's dinner.

I swear they must have been able to hear Lana's anguished scream all the way down in Battery Park City.

As if that weren't perfect enough, as Lana was calling Josh terrible names for wrecking his groin on their first Valentine's Day as a couple, the Guy Who Hates It When They Put Corn in the Chili came by with his tray, and Lana flung out one arm a little too dramatically, and hit the Guy Who Hates It When They Put Corn in the Chili's tray, and his taco salad went sailing through the air, and ended up all over Lana.

Seriously. *There was salsa in her hair.*

What could Tina and I do but high-five each other?

But amazingly, things got even BETTER after that. Because Michael actually skipped his Computer Club meeting to sit next to me!!!!!

I couldn't believe it, but suddenly, there he was, saying he obviously couldn't trust the male population of Albert Einstein High School not to scam on his girlfriend while his back was turned, so he was going to guard me with his life!!!! Because of Kenny and the Whitman's Sampler!!!!!!

Which I thought was so cute—even though, okay, as a feminist I should have been offended because, of course, I don't need any man to defend me from the unwanted advances of others, since I am perfectly capable of applying a well-placed heel to the testicular area, like Lars showed me that time we were doing krav maga self-defense techniques in the event someone should try to kidnap me—I suddenly forgot all about my shyness over giving him the Valentine I'd made, and my fears over how dorky he—and everyone else at my lunch table—might think it is. Instead, I just pulled it out of my backpack, and handed it to him.

And my mom was right!!!!! MICHAEL TOTALLY LOVED IT!!!!!

Of course, it wasn't just an ORDINARY Valentine: It was a little book I made, with tear-out coupons for things Michael can ask me to do, like take Pavlov for a walk, or give him a neck massage (Michael, not Pavlov), or kiss him (I put in, like, four of those!!!). All Michael has to do when he wants me to do one of these things is rip out the coupon and hand it to me. Which he did right away (one of the kiss coupons).

So we practically made out at the lunch table until Lars and Tina's bodyguard, Wahim, started clearing their throats, and Lilly was all, "OH, GOD. GET A ROOM!"

Mom was right: The point of Valentine's Day ISN'T what you get, but what you give. TOTALLY.

Oh my God, it was so great.

Um, well, except for the part right after that when Boris—I guess inspired by Michael's reaction to my Valentine—suddenly took his violin out of its case and, IN FRONT OF EVERYONE, started playing "The Music of the Night" from *The Phantom of the Opera,* inching closer and closer to Lilly, until finally his bow was all up in her face, and we looked at the end of it, and dangling from it was the genuine simulated ruby heart pendant from Kay Jewelers.

And Lilly, instead of being all, "Aw, thanks, Boris, how sweet," was like, "What's THIS?" and "How did THAT get on your bow?"

And Boris finally had to stop playing and be like, "Happy Valentine's Day, Lilly. It's for you. I hope you like it."

And Lilly was all, "Oh my God, you actually got me that dorky necklace from Kay's?" with this big smirk on her face.

I couldn't believe it! Even now it pains me to have to record that my best friend would say something so cruel. Tina went white as a sheet, and Michael looked angry, and poor Boris looked as if he'd been slapped!

So I went, "Oh my God, Boris, it's so beautiful!" and "That was so thoughtful of him, wasn't it, Lilly?" while kicking her VERY HARD beneath the lunch table.

And finally Lilly, after giving me a bunch of dirty looks and going, "What?" like ten times, went, "Oh. Yeah. Thanks, Boris. That was nice. But, you know, I don't really approve of gemstones because of the conditions under which the people who mine them in Africa have to live."

"They're simulated," Tina explained to her, in a strangled voice.

And Lilly just went, "Oh."

But by that time Boris had put his violin away and slunk off.

"Nice job," Michael said to his sister sarcastically.

But Lilly just got all indignant, and went, "Oh, whatever! Like you got your girlfriend anything!"

And Michael was like, "I tell Mia I love her every day. I don't need some greeting card company reminding me to say it once a year. How often do you tell Boris you care about *him*?"

And Lilly turned all red and excused herself.

But I think Lilly must have apologized, and the two of them have made up already, because Lilly let herself into the supply closet a little while ago, where Boris was practicing, and I haven't heard a sound out of there ever since.

Still, it was hard to meet Tina's gaze after that, because she's been wanting one of those heart necklaces for, like, ever.

So I said, to make her feel better, as we were heading back to class, "I'll come to your Audrey Hepburn movie marathon tonight, Tina, if the invitation is still open."

And she totally cheered up. Especially when I gave her my Whitman's Sampler. Because Lilly is right: I really don't like the cream-filled kind.

Friday, February 14, French

Michael just caught me in the hall and tried to hand me one of my "Dinner with Mia" coupons.

"Let's go out tonight," he said. "For a romantic Valentine's Day dinner. I know you won't believe it, but I got reservations at One if by Land, Two if by Sea. I guess they had a cancelation or something."

He was right. I *couldn't* believe it.

And the worst part was, he looked so cute—so handsome and hopeful—standing there with my coupon in his hand, and just the beginning of a five o'clock shadow on his neck.

But I had to say, "I'm sorry, Michael. But I already made plans with Tina. She's having a Valentine's Day slumber party, and you never said anything about doing anything together, so I told her I'd go."

Because no way was I canceling on Tina the way Lana had on Trish. I don't want any bad karma coming back at ME!

His face fell. "You're kidding me."

"Well, you kept going on about how you didn't even believe in Valentine's Day, so I just figured—"

"I know!" he said, laughing. "I know, I know! I'm an idiot, all right? It's just . . . I'm not used to having a girlfriend."

SO TINA WAS RIGHT!!!! It wasn't that Michael had anything against Valentine's Day. He'd just never had a reason to celebrate it before!!!

"Listen," he went on. "Will you go out with me tomorrow night, then?"

"I'd be delighted to," I said.

"Good," Michael said gravely, tucking the coupon into my hand. "I'm going to make this one Lupercalia dinner you'll never forget."

And I remembered what he'd said about the ancient Roman feast of February 15.

"Maybe Lupercalia will be our private Valentine's Day," I said. "From now on."

"Deal," Michael said.

And kissed me. Right in the hallway. Where Mr. G or Principal Gupta could have seen.

But I didn't care, because I was so happy.

I'm not going to end up with a Leo—or KENNY—after all!!!!!!!!!!!!

Ha!!! Take THAT, Dr. Steve!

Friday, February 14, the Plaza

Well, Grandmère's back. I knew it was too good to last.

When I walked into her suite, I didn't see her at first, even though I knew she was there because I called ahead this time. It turns out the reason I didn't see her was because she was stretched out on the couch in a cream-colored peignoir, a Sidecar and ashtray within reach, and her leg in an enormous air cast.

"Oh my God, Grandmère," I yelled. "What happened to you? Did you get a groin injury, too?"

"For God's sakes, stop yelling, Amelia," she said, looking pained. "What are you talking about, groin injury? Haven't I ever told you princesses don't talk about groins?"

"Um, sorry," I said, looking around. But there was no sign of Dr. Steve. Was it possible—were Grandmère and I *alone*? Well, I mean, except for Rommel, who was curled up next to Grandmère's non-broken foot. "But what happened?"

"I don't want to talk about it," Grandmère said.

"Pull up a chair and sit down. Today I want to go over what to do in the event that you are ever trapped in conversation by an autograph seeker. Obviously you don't want to alienate the person, because as a royal it doesn't pay to make enemies—even people who are only going to sell your signature on eBay. But it can become frustrating when someone, enamored of your celebrity, won't shut up. So the excuse to leave that I've always found most helpful is the following: *I beg your pardon, but I believe I see the Comte de Rosti over there. I simply must go say hello, I haven't seen him since last season in Biarritz—*"

"Grandmère," I interrupted. Even though princesses don't interrupt. "Are you going to tell me what happened to your foot, or not?" Then I suddenly remembered something. And my blood went cold. "Oh my God, Grandmère! Dr. Steve was right! He predicted that you were going to sustain a grievous bodily injury!"

Which meant he might be right about his OTHER predictions as well—like that I'm going to end up with a LEO after all!!!! Oh, no!

But then Grandmère said, in a scathing tone, "Dr. Steve! Never mention that name to me again!"

"But, Grandmère!" I actually felt kind of sick. Because if Grandmère actually HAD sustained a grievous bodily injury, then what were the chances that Dr. Steve's prediction about me was going to come true as well????? "He said—"

"I sustained this injury FLEEING from that man's odious advances!" Grandmère cried. "Imagine my horror when, after inviting him up for coffee and petits fours following his performance on that nice Mr. Letterman's television show, that so-called doctor suddenly began insisting he had feelings for me! *Romantic* feelings! I told him he had to be mistaken—that he was confusing his gratitude for all that I had done for him with love. But he wouldn't believe me! He kept clinging to my hand and talking about how happy we two were going to be when we were married and living in Genovia!"

I had to try really hard to keep a straight face.

"Well, Grandmère," I said. "I mean, you two *have* been spending an awful lot of time together this week. You can understand if the guy thought maybe there was more to it than simple friendship—"

"Amelia!" Grandmère looked horrified. "Are you joking? I'm a princess, and he's . . . he's . . . a commoner! Of all the impertinence! I have never in my life heard of anything so ridiculous! Of course I told him so at once, but the impudent cuss thought I was playing hard to get! He actually tried to *kiss* me, Amelia!" Grandmère had to take a sip of her Sidecar to fortify herself before she could go on.

Meanwhile, I was trying so hard not to laugh, tears were practically streaming down my face.

"Well, of course I slapped him for his insolence," Grandmère explained. "And what do you think he did? Seized me by the arms and told me I light a fire in him unlike any other woman he has ever known. As if I haven't heard *that* line before! The horrible man couldn't think of an original thing to say if his TROUSERS were exploding! Of course I screamed for Raoul"—Raoul is Grandmère's bodyguard—"and he came rushing in, but not before I'd managed to break free myself. But then I accidentally tripped over poor Rommel, who was trying frantically to come to my rescue. Which is how I broke my toe. I'm going to have to speak to Gucci about this season's kitten heels; they are simply *too* high. . . ."

"Still," I said, struggling not to crack up. "The guy was right about two of his predictions . . . you *did* sustain grievous bodily harm, and a man *did* propose to you. . . ."

Grandmère gave me a very sour look. "I suppose you think you're amusing. Well, you might as well make yourself useful, and go and get me some Tylenol. And fix me another Sidecar, this one's gone warm. . . ."

I got up to do as Grandmère asked. I figured it was the least I could do, since she'd been through so much. True, most of it was her own fault . . . but there are lots of different kinds of Valentines, and I figured that mine to Grandmère would be that I would never speak of Dr. Steve to her—or anyone else—ever again.

And to tell you the truth, this seemed to suit Grandmère even better than a heart-shaped box of chocolates or a simulated ruby heart pendant.

!!!!!!!!!!!!!!

Tonight as I was getting my stuff together to go to Tina's, I heard this weird tapping noise. ON MY WINDOW.

At first I thought it was a pigeon. But then I looked out and got the scare—and delight—of my life:

MICHAEL WAS ON MY FIRE ESCAPE!!!!

I couldn't believe it! I ran over to the window and flung it open and was like, "WHAT ARE YOU DOING HERE???? WHY ARE YOU ON THE FIRE ESCAPE???? WHY DIDN'T YOU RING THE DOOR BUZZER LIKE A NORMAL PERSON?????"

But he just smiled and said, "It's more romantic this way."

"But how did you even get out there?" I demanded. Because Lars worked really hard at securing the entrance to our building's courtyard, which is what my bedroom looks out over, so that no one could do what Michael had—crawl up to my window via the fire escape.

Michael smiled even more and said, "Your neighbor Ronnie let me out here. Now stop talking. I know you have to go to Tina's in a minute, but I wanted to give you your Lupercalia gift before you leave. I realize it's a day early, but I couldn't wait."

And that's when he picked up his guitar and there, in the light from the security lamp, he serenaded me with "our song"—the one he wrote about me, "Tall Drink of Water," which goes:

> *Tall drink of water*
> *Can't say how much you want her*
> *How long you've tried to stay cool*
> *But she doesn't even see you*
>
> *Wait for her in the lobby*
> *Your knees are getting wobbly*

She glides by in her pink dress
Towers over all the rest
Hands starting to get sweaty
You really think you're ready
To take a little walk over there
Tell her how much you care

What will you say now
Will she make your day now
She looks this way now
Get moving, don't delay now

You think you're ready for your close-up
But she's not China doll made-up
Or a picture-perfect teacup
She's more real than any girl you've ever seen

You're not gonna make it
But this is it, you just can't fake it
She's the girl who makes your heart sing
Means more to you than anything

She's a tall drink of water
Can't say how much you want her
How long you've tried to stay cool
But she doesn't even see you

And it was the best Valentine I ever got.

ME, A PRINCESS???? YEAH, RIGHT.
A Screenplay by Mia Thermopolis
(first draft)

Scene 45

INT/NIGHT—A girl (sixteen-year-old MIA THER-
MOPOLIS), trembling on the verge of womanhood,
sits in a sumptuous leather seat aboard a luxurious
private jet. She has just finished reading the contents
of a black-and-white Mead composition notebook.
She closes the notebook, looks up, and sighs.

MIA

And Michael and I have had happy Valentine's
Days ever since. . . .

Oh, whatever, that isn't even true. Michael
STILL refuses to celebrate Valentine's Day, insisting it's all a plot by Hallmark, 1-800-Flowers, and

Russell Stover to make us do their corporate bidding.

But he doesn't mind celebrating Lupercalia on February 15.

Except that they don't make Happy Lupercalia cards. Which I'm pretty sure is why he likes it so much.

And, I have to admit—so do I!